# THE ATTIC

Book 2

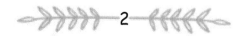

# TABLE OF CONTENTS

CHAPTER 1

Sleepless Nights ............................................................5

CHAPTER 2

The First Omen ..............................................................9

CHAPTER 3

Trial and Error ..............................................................12

CHAPTER 3

Calling in Reinforcements .........................................18

CHAPTER 3

The Magic Shop ...........................................................23

CHAPTER 6

A Narrow Escape .........................................................30

CHAPTER 7

Well-Needed Rest........................................................35

CHAPTER 8

The Second Omen........................................................39

CHAPTER 9

Hope at Last.................................................................43

CHAPTER 10

All for Nothing .............................................................49

# CHAPTER 1

## Sleepless Nights

Somewhere nearby, a branch snapped. Richard shuddered, tucking his legs closer to his body beneath his hoodie. The chill he felt could've easily been from fear or from the cold. His home for the night was a tunnel made from thick plastic at a local playground not far off from his school. The size was small enough that even at his age, he found it a little cramped — but that was good as it made Richard feel more hidden.

That security didn't stop him from holding his breath as he tried to identify the source of the noise. Human, or animal? His heart began to beat faster. It has been a few weeks since he went on the run, and it was getting harder and harder to avoid the people searching for him. During the day he couldn't stop moving, and at night, he couldn't let himself feel too safe.

It isn't just the living that he had to worry about. Richard thought that taking the book away from his house was the answer, but he was beginning to realize he was in a much deeper problem than he imagined.

The sound of shuffling was getting closer, and with it, Richard's heart raced even harder. The sound got louder, too loud, like twigs were cracking inside of his ears, and Richard had to clamp his hands over them to try and block out the noise. It was impossible; he had to be imagining things. Closing his eyes, he counted in his head to ten, and the sound faded into silence.

He opened his eyes. The spirit was crouched in the entrance of the tunnel, it was smiling, teeth gray and rotting. BAM! The spirit lunged at him before he could so much as suck in a breath. A flash of cold dirt and squirming bugs filled his brain, and Richard nearly screamed, but it was gone just as fast, as was the vision of the spirit. Outside of the tunnel, a raccoon was strolling lazily past. Letting out a breath of relief and exhaustion, Richard fell backwards against the tunnel, resting his head.

He wouldn't be sleeping much again that night, he knew it. The little amount of rest he'd been getting was plagued by terror, and that was enough to let him know that whatever he'd unleashed from the book wasn't going to let him get away so easily. There was nowhere he could run, nowhere he could hide, and leaving it for someone else to stumble upon was dangerous and irresponsible. As long as this relic of dark magic existed, someone would be at risk.

When he took out all the other options, the solution was surprisingly simple: it had to be destroyed.

# CHAPTER 2

## The First Omen

All around him, Salem burned. Richard stumbled forward in a panicked daze, knowing where he had to go. As he ran, a chorus of screaming, wailing, and sinister laughter filled his ears. The night sky was orange, the moon red, and not a single star was visible through the layer of smoke that had overtaken the city. His lungs burned and he couldn't stop himself from coughing as he ran, but nonetheless, Richard pushed on.

Past the school, past the shops, past the row of little homes, past the sting of his own tears in his drying eyes and his weakening legs. Down the dirt road that led up the hill, to the house where it all began. *His* house. And there it was, at the top, flames shooting from every shattered window. Richard watched in horror, knowing that going inside was certain death. Still, he felt compelled to continue onward, toward the front steps, to fling open the door and that should've been that.

Richard expected to burn. For heat to lick at his face and his clothes to light up and take him with it. If he could still push forward and find his family, that would be enough. This was all his fault, he had to be there with them in the end. But when he shouldered his way inside, there was no fire. There was heat, the kind that made your hair and your clothes stick to your skin, and even after just a few seconds, he could feel droplets begin to form at the sides of his face.

All in all, it was like what Richard imagined it must be like to be stuck inside of an oven, but aside from that, looking around showed nothing out of the ordinary. All the lights were off in the house.

"Dad? Debbie?"

No answer. He stepped forward and something crunched under his shoe. Glass. Looking up, Richard could see that the ceiling lights were all broken; so no use trying a switch.

Footsteps thumped upstairs. A door slammed.

Somehow, he knew it was the attic door. And not just that, but something *wanted* him to go up there.

At this point, Richard woke up, clammy with sweat.

It was the same nightmare he'd had for the past week, only each time, he got closer to the attic.

# CHAPTER 3

## Trial and Error

Each day of the week, Richard had been learning, it came with its own ups and downs. On a weekend, nobody looked twice at a boy his age roaming around on his own, but there were more chances someone was going to recognize him from the broadcasts and posters. On a weekday, he could move around more freely if he steered clear of the adults that might stop to question why he isn't in school.

This would've been easier in New York. There were way more people, and they were way too busy and bustling about to notice one stray kid. In fact, you'd be hard pressed to go far without seeing other kids who probably should've been in school. Salem, Massachusetts was different. It was a smaller, more tightly knit community. Word traveled fast here, and Richard had too many close calls.

His saving grace had come in the form of a pawn shop run by an elderly man who had failing eyesight and rarely got up from behind the service desk, where he had a small TV stationed. Richard had been living off what allowance he still had left in his backpack and had been able to get plenty for cheap at this place, like a new set of clothes other than the last ones he was seen in when he ran away. That, and there was a vending machine. The store owner never asked questions, and Richard had a feeling he simply didn't notice anything amiss.

Today, his purchases served one purpose: destroying the spell book. He found an old lighter, a can of spray paint, and a bottle of rubbing alcohol. It cost him most of what he had left of his dwindling funds, but at least he had enough left to snag himself a bottle of water and a bag of trail mix. That would be breakfast. Hopefully, that would be all he needed. If this worked, he could head home. Whatever happened afterward was going to be hard, but at least the worst would have passed. Once he'd made this right, the rest would follow.

With his materials secured, Richard made his way to a concrete ravine he'd discovered early on in his travels. It wasn't his favorite place to be. The puddles smelled foul and the underside of the bridge was covered in graffiti. It reminded him of New York in the worst possible kind of way, and he had a feeling that coming out here after dark would be asking for trouble. It was still mid-morning, though, and sure enough, he found it empty.

Opening the book was a last resort. Richard pulled it from his backpack and set it on the ground in front of him. Even closed, it menaced him with its silver emblem. *It's just a book,* he reminded himself. *An evil book, sure, but it can't do anything to you by itself.*

Sure, he didn't know how true that was, but unless he at least believed in that much, he'd never be able to go through with this. Now was no time for doubting.

Fire, first. Cautiously, Richard flicked on the lighter and held it to the edge of the book's cover. Nothing. It wouldn't light. Disappointing, but not all that surprising. That was why he came prepared with other options. Richard took the cap off the rubbing alcohol and doused the book. Again, he tried to set it ablaze, but even adding the flammable liquid made no difference.

Right, so it was time to go in. Holding his breath, Richard closed his eyes and threw the cover open. For what he wanted to do, he didn't need to risk getting his mind hijacked. Grabbing fistfuls of the aged parchment, Richard ripped and tore at them. Or, at least, he tried to.

His fingers went limp as soon as he tried to pull at the pages, allowing them to fall freely back in place. Several attempts only gave the same result. Each time, the paper slipped between his fingers, unharmed. Letting out a groan of frustration, Richard slammed the book shut again. His last resort: the paint. If he couldn't physically destroy the book, he figured he could at least make it completely unreadable.

For a moment, it seemed as if it worked. The thick paint easily covered over the parchment, and Richard was confident that if he worked fast, he could coat every page before they dried, causing the whole book to solidify into a useless brick. It wasn't fun work, especially since Richard was doing his best to make sure he didn't look directly at any of the pages, and it felt like he was going to run out of paint at any given time, but before long, the deed was done.

Richard sat back and admired his work. His fingers were stained with paint, but the book sat there coated. It was over. Or so he thought.

The book was about to show him exactly how tough it was.

# CHAPTER 4

## Calling in Reinforcements

Just as Richard was about to celebrate his victory, the book began to hiss and sizzle. He felt the color leave his face as he looked on in horror. The paint was *boiling*. And not just that, but lifting itself in heated bubbles from each page, evaporating into the air. He couldn't do anything but watch, transfixed, as each inch of paint he'd used removed itself from the pages of the spell book until, finally, it closed itself and sat there in perfect condition, like he'd never done anything to it in the first place.

He could've screamed. He wanted to pick it up and throw it into the nearest ditch, but what good would hiding it do? Eventually, someone would find it – that much he was sure of. And if he couldn't burn it or rip it or ruin it, he was sure that anything else he tried would be just as useless. Richard's head hurt. He was exhausted, in over his head, and completely out of ideas. Talking to anyone was a risk, but at this point, he could use all the help he could get.

It was time to reach out to his one ally.

***

Richard caught Harvey on his way out of school for the day. He tried not to get too close, lest any of the staff or parents picking up their kids recognized him, but he knew that Harvey walked home, and wearing a backpack, it was easy enough for him to get written off as just another student walking home with a friend or a neighbor. As soon as Harvey saw him, he took the side closest to the road, using his bigger size to provide cover.

It wasn't the first time that he'd met with Harvey, though he only did it when it was absolutely necessary. The older boy knew what he was going through, and although he didn't like the idea of Richard being away from home for so long, he understood why Richard made that decision. It was just nice to have someone on his side; it made Richard feel much less crazy.

"You look terrible," Harvey said with a frown. "When was the last time you ate something more than what you find in a vending machine?"

"That's not what's killing me." Richard explained how hard it was getting for him to sleep through the night: that he was having nightmares, and sometimes seeing ghosts, like the hauntings were catching up to him even though he'd left the house.

"It's got to be the book." Harvey glanced toward Richard's backpack, knowing it was in there. "It must be strongest when it's in that house, but still have plenty of power on its own."

Richard nodded, rubbing his eyes with his palms. "You're telling me." He grumbled, explaining what he'd spent the better part of the day doing. "I already tried everything."

For a while, the two of them were silent. Nothing passed between them but the sound of their shoes crunching the scattered leaves on the pavement until all at once Harvey snapped up, face animated.

"No," he said, "not quite everything."

Richard shot him an impatient look. This wasn't any time to build up suspense!

"Have you tried fighting fire with fire?"

"I've tried fire," Richard started, but Harvey shook his head.

"No," he explained, "I mean, maybe the only way to take out a *magic* book is...well, with more magic!"

Richard had to admit that it made sense, but it didn't make him any less frustrated. He sighed, shoulders sagging. "Okay, sure, but the last time I checked, neither of us know anything about magic. I don't think abracadabra is going to cut it."

Laughing, Harvey swung an arm around Richard's shoulder, giving him a confident look.

"Time for you to learn just a bit more about Salem's rich history."

# CHAPTER 5

## The Magic Shop

Turns out, there were a decent amount of townsfolk who leaned into the fame of the whole "witch trials" thing. History marked the city as the site of one of America's worst tragedies, where hundreds of innocent people lost their lives due to false claims of witchcraft. Richard's experience told him that there was more to it than that: real witches had been among the people all along, and there was no way to know now how many. Even though this was nothing to boast about, tourists still arrived frequently to look at the memorial for the lives lost, as well as other historical points of interest in town.

That was where the magic shop came in. When Harvey told him about it, Richard couldn't help but doubt. To him, a magic shop was a place where you could find cheap props that taught kids sleight of hand and other performance tricks, but Harvey had assured him that this was different. The older boy had to go home to check in with his Mom, but gave Richard a quick set of directions and promised to meet him there as soon as he could.

"You can't miss it," he said before the two of them branched off in different directions. He'd been right.

Richard knew which building it was as soon as it came into view. It was the only shop that was completely black. It sat on the corner of the street in a way that made it separate from the ones around it, and the building itself was clearly old: a one-time home that had been renovated into the business it was today. A big sign at the edge of the lot even boasted it as a plot of land that was full of history. Well, it certainly looked like the real deal, at least, but if anything in there could help was another question entirely.

A bell chimed overhead as Richard went inside. The store was thick with an aroma of different things from nature that he couldn't identify, and made him a little light-headed, but he figured he'd get used to it before long. It was hard not to gawk. All around him, the different wares begged to be looked at.

There were animal skeletons, crystals in different shapes and sizes, books on witchcraft, tarot cards, black candles, and wreaths made from sticks. It was kind of awesome, but some of the charm was lost on Richard because of his recent experiences. Harvey had promised him that this kind of practiced magic mostly involved things like palm reading and predicting your future through cards, but Richard didn't know enough about these things to feel particularly safe.

At least, not until the shopkeeper came out from a doorway to the back. Everything about her put him at ease immediately, from her bushy red hair and her huge glasses to her cat-print dress and knit cardigan. She reminded him of a grade-school teacher, and she smiled as she came over.

"Hello, hello! Fresh out of school, young man? Need a charm to clear your head and get you through the next big test? I've got just the thing!" She turned, looking like she was about to head off to a part of the shop, chattering all the way, so Richard cleared his throat and stepped forward to explain.

"Actually," he said, "I have a different problem I was hoping you could help me with."

"Oh?"

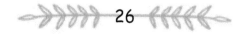

A glint of curiosity filled her round face as he swung his backpack around to retrieve the spell book. Richard had the feeling that she didn't get a lot of kids with unique problems. As far as he was concerned, that was all for the better. When he could go back to worrying about long division, he'd be grateful.

Richard pulled the book clear from its hiding place, and as soon as the shopkeeper laid eyes on it, her entire expression transformed. Her face went pale, and her hands shook as she reached out for it.

"May I?"

He nodded, handing it over. She held it between her fingers like it was a snake: beautiful and relaxed, but something that could still bite her at any given moment if she handled it wrong. Richard felt relieved; she already knew just how dangerous this was. She knew that it was the real thing...and so, there was no way she'd think he was crazy, either.

"Young man," she said, speaking slowly, "I don't know how you came across such a terrible book, but I have a feeling you've already run afoul of the evil it holds."

Exhausted, he only slumped his shoulders in response before asking the one thing that mattered:

"Can you help me get rid of it?"

The shopkeeper looked up from the spell book to give him a kind smile and reached out to put a hand on his shoulder. "Of course," she promised. "Powerful black magic like this is better off lost to time; you wouldn't want it ending up in the wrong hands. Why don't you take a seat at the table by the window? You look like you could use a hot cup of tea to boost your spirits, and then we'll get down to business."

Richard couldn't help but smile. Truthfully, tea did sound nice. So did getting off his feet for a few minutes.

He was halfway there when a loud crash came from somewhere in the back room. The shopkeeper was already heading that way, but in her alarm, placed the spell book on the service counter before rushing back to see what had happened. A black cat yowled and ran out when she opened the door and disappeared behind it, hair all on end and back hunched. It sounded like something big had broken, and Richard was just about to go and see if she needed any help when a red-faced Harvey burst in through the front door.

# CHAPTER 6

# A Narrow Escape

"No time," he said before Richard could open his mouth. Harvey whipped his head around frantically, his eyes falling on the abandoned spell book. The older boy grabbed it with one hand and grabbed Richard's arm with the other, pulling them both outside. "I'll explain in a minute, just run!"

The look on Harvey's face left no room for questioning. Richard did what he was told, breaking out into a sprint that would use up all the energy he had left. Ahead of him, Harvey made an abrupt turn, darting into an alleyway between two restaurants. It happened so fast that Richard nearly fell over trying to change directions.

Harvey yanked him down behind a dumpster, spell book gripped tightly to his chest, and the two pressed themselves to the wall and crouched, breathless.

"What was that about?" Richard asked between gasps for air, but Harvey just shook his head, slumping down further.

Fast approaching was the sound of sirens. Police cars whizzed past their hiding spot in the direction that they'd just come from. Richard was too dazed to understand the significance until Harvey finally caught his breath and spoke.

"She knew," he said. "The woman from the magic store. She knew who you were."

It didn't make sense. She'd reported him to the police? But she'd been with him the whole time and had been so nice. It was Richard's turn to shake his head, but even as he did, things began to click into place.

She hadn't been in the main part of the store when he'd initially come inside. He'd had a few moments to browse, which would have been more than enough time for her to make a phone call if she'd caught a glimpse of him and recognized that he was the missing boy all over the news. That was why she'd wanted him to sit; she wasn't being nice. She was stalling for time. Richard felt like an idiot.

Harvey seemed to read the look on his face and put a hand on his shoulder. "It's not your fault. I had no idea, either. I always thought she was just...kind of quirky, you know?"

That only inspired more questions. "Wait, what do you mean? Anyone would've turned me in."

Harvey's look got severe, and he pulled out a folded piece of computer paper from his pocket. "I was doing a quick search to see if I could find anything helpful online before heading over, and I found this."

He handed it over, and Richard unfolded the paper. It was an old photo of a few women smiling outside of the magic shop. The shopkeeper was in the center. There was nothing particularly odd or concerning about the photo that he could see and was about to question Harvey further...when he saw it. It was such a small detail; he almost missed it completely.

There, around the shopkeeper's neck, was a pendant. It was silver, with the head of a goat. The same emblem that could be seen on the front of the spell book. The one that glared at him from Harvey's lap. Richard thought about the look on the woman's face when she took the book from him. He'd thought it was horror, but thinking about it now, he realized his mistake. She had been in awe.

And she had set him up.

# CHAPTER 7

## Well-Needed Rest

They couldn't stay where they were. It would only be so long before the police started to search the area for a trace of the missing boy that had been reported just a few moments prior. Deciding it couldn't be helped, Harvey decided to sneak Richard home with him.

Richard had tried protesting, but Harvey had shut him down with a teasing, "come on, when was the last time you took a shower?"

It was a point that he couldn't really argue.

So, the two made a careful trip to Harvey's house, where Harvey directed Richard to go around back, through the garage, while he distracted his mom and sister in the kitchen. From there, he was easily able to make his way unseen to the staircase and then to Harvey's room. It was tempting to throw himself onto the bed but he settled for the floor. The carpet alone was such a welcome change that he would've fallen asleep in minutes if Harvey hadn't followed up straight behind him.

The woman who ran the magic shop had been a dead end, leaving the question of how to get rid of the spell book back at square one. Harvey told his parents he needed to study, and took his dinner into his room, where the extra-large portion he brought with him was shared with Richard. They tried to brainstorm the next step, but all ideas came back to needing to fight magic with magic. And that, they didn't know how to do — or who they could trust, for that matter.

If he was being totally honest, it was a little hard for Richard to focus on anything beyond the hot food he was eating, anyway. It was too nice to have a fresh, solid meal. It was too nice being inside again. Harvey caught on quick and proclaimed that the rest of the night would be an official break from all things involving evil spirits. With his declaration, Richard allowed himself to relax.

There was ice cream, a hot shower, clean clothes (pajamas!), and a pillow and blanket to curl up with. They talked about their favorite video games and cartoons, and Harvey said he'd teach Richard how to skateboard once everything went back to normal. It was nice to talk to him like a friend instead of just someone who could help him escape a supernatural force determined to destroy him.

It was such a welcome change of pace that Richard found he didn't want to fall asleep at all.

Unfortunately, his body knew what it needed, and Richard drifted off much sooner than he wanted, still smiling as he listened to Harvey talk about his classmates.

# CHAPTER 8

## The Second Omen

Once again, Salem was burning. Richard had no choice but to follow his dream-destined path through the town, up to his house at the top of the hill. Once again, he pushed into the building that appeared to be up in flames, only to find it unharmed inside. Once again, he noticed the glass from the broken lights on the floor, and once again, realized that someone, or something, was waiting for him in the attic.

The nightmare continued. Richard made his way to the staircase and scaled it step-by-step, like he couldn't help but do it. His whole body hurt from the running he'd done, his head was foggy, and his heart hammered in fear. The closer he got to the attic, the worse he felt, but there was no stopping his feet from continuing forward. No matter how scared he was, there just wasn't anywhere else for him to go. Whatever was waiting for him, he had to face it head-on.

By the time he reached the foot of the narrow stairway that led to the attic, Richard could make out low voices coming from behind the door above him. It sounded almost like singing, but he couldn't be sure. It was hard to make out over the sound of his heart beating in his ears. With each step up the staircase, the sense of dread he felt grew stronger, so by the time his hand was reaching for the doorknob, he could barely stomach the idea of going inside.

Still, that's exactly what he did.

Inside, a group of hooded figures chanted something in a language Richard couldn't identify, but that made him feel sick and dizzy. The old furniture that had once been scattered inside the attic had been cleared away, and the darkness was washed in a red glow coming from strange symbols that had been carved into the floor. But the worst and most terrible of it all was what was in the very center of the room.

His Dad and Stepmom were standing there, eyes glazed as if in a daze, and his newborn baby brother was cradled carefully in her arms. The baby was crying, trying to get his mother's attention, but the two adults were deaf to the rest of the world, too caught in the magical trap that had been laid out for them. And who were all these people? Why were they doing this?

Richard swayed. His knees felt like they were going to give out, but before he could fall, hands reached out and braced him by the arms.

They weren't human hands.

They were too long, too thin, with blackened skin and curling nails. Richard couldn't bring himself to turn his head and look to see what it was, but in a voice that was stuck somewhere between a hiss and a croak, it whispered into his ear: *"Are you enjoying this glimpse into your future?"*

# CHAPTER 9

## Hope at Last

When Richard woke up, Harvey's alarm was ringing. Looking over, the older boy seemed too dazed to turn it off. The two of them just stared at each other for a long moment, and somehow, Richard knew the answer before he'd even asked. It was something about the look on his face.

"Did you dream about..."

Harvey gave a solemn nod and turned off his alarm. "Yeah," he said, "I did."

No further explanation was necessary. Whatever break they'd had last night was officially over. If that dream really was a look into the future, they couldn't afford to waste any more time. Harvey had to get to school but promised that he'd use his breaks to do what research he could on his phone.

Meanwhile, Richard would continue his own search. Harvey offered to leave his laptop password for him to use while he was at school, but Richard had a better idea. He had a feeling that the answers they needed lay somewhere in the city, and there was one place that made the most sense to check: the local library. The popularized version of the city's history could be found anywhere, but if there were going to be any different accounts, maybe from former residents of Salem themselves, that was his best bet.

If he couldn't find anything there, Richard didn't know where he was going to find the answers that he needed.

He waited until the house was obviously empty before he left the way that he entered, out the back door, and snuck onto the street. It was still early, so he hoped anyone who saw him just assumed he was running late on his way to school. Harvey had lent him more clothes, so the ones he'd been wearing when he was reported the day before couldn't give him away.

Unsurprisingly, the old library was virtually empty when he got there. He'd seen busy libraries before, living in New York, but a city like this didn't have enough people with the free time during your average weekday to spend it browsing the stacks for their next favorite read. The only sound was that of the librarian at the front desk stamping something systematically into the front pages of an intimidatingly large stack of books she had piled on her desk. She didn't so much as glance his way when he came in, so he had a feeling that she hadn't even noticed him.

That was all for the better, anyway. Richard found a table squirreled away in a far corner of the building, sheltered by the tall bookshelves, and set his backpack on one of the chairs. The local history section was nearby, and right away, he felt his heart skip with hope. The small section had books of varying sizes and publication dates, but most of them were decently old, and some almost looked like they were little more than journals that had been donated for the purpose of being a community resource.

There was one title in particular that caught his attention. It was a slim and frayed hardcover book that had to have been one-of-a-kind, and judging by the dust that had accumulated on the top, hadn't been touched by anyone in ages. There was no author credited that he could find, but the words on the cover spoke for themselves: *'Salem's Restless Souls'*

A brief look inside told Richard that he had found exactly what he needed. He doubted that the book would answer all of his questions about what was happening to him, but what it *did* have was a section with the title: "What to do when the dead have been disturbed; Re-introducing peace into the home."

He wouldn't know for sure, of course, until he gave it a full read, so he took the book back with him to his table...and that's where his excitement came crashing down. His backpack was open; and he was sure he hadn't left it that way. In his haste to check on it, he almost fell over, just to discover his worst fear had been realized: it was gone. *The spell book was gone.*

But who? How? He'd only been away for a minute or two, and he hadn't noticed anyone around other than the librarian, and she was busy with...no, that was wrong. Richard couldn't hear the stamp anymore. The library was fully quiet, now.

And what was worse? Now that he stood there in a panic, he was noticing things he hadn't, before. Namely, the architecture of the library. It featured columns that curved into leaping, dark-eyed rams at the ceiling.

Without having had any way of knowing, he'd walked right into an ambush.

# CHAPTER 10

## All for Nothing

He had to get out of here. Richard slipped the book in his hands into his backpack and zipped it shut. Reaching the lobby, he could feel the librarian's eyes on him, watching his every movement. A part of him was tempted to walk right up to her and accuse her of stealing, but what would that accomplish? There was no way he'd get the book back by making a scene, and if what happened the day before was anything to go by, she'd already alerted the police that he was here.

Not taking his eyes off her, Richard backed up until he was out of sight in the book stacks once again. He'd try the emergency exit; there was bound to be one somewhere on the other side of the building. If he went out the front, he knew there'd be someone waiting for him. It was likely that using the emergency exit would trigger an alarm, but he'd just have to run as soon as he made it out.

Once he had the exit in sight, Richard picked up speed until he had his hand on the handle. He took a deep breath, bracing himself for the alarm...but couldn't push it open. A firm hand was on his shoulder, and in his surprise, Richard whirled around to find himself face-to-chest with a mountainous police officer.

"Come on, now, son," he said. "A lot of people have been mighty worried about you."

It was stupid, but Richard felt his stomach churn with shame, his face growing hot. He hung his head. He'd been caught. His weeks on the run were over, and he had nothing to show for it.

The officer led him out through the front, where a crowd of curious citizens had gathered to peek at what was going on. It looked like the whole police force had come to surround the building, and Richard couldn't bring himself to look anyone in the face. He knew what they were all thinking: he was troubled. The sort of questioning his parents were going to go through, and probably already had been going through, made him feel impossibly guilty. He'd felt that way since he had resolved to run, but now that it was all crashing down around him, he couldn't ignore it anymore.

It wasn't until he was secured in the back of the officer's car that he dared to look out the back window. He was both hoping and dreading to see his parents arriving. He missed them, but he knew that they weren't going to be happy to see him. They'd be relieved, of course, but undoubtedly angry and confused and hurt. Richard didn't get that far.

His gaze stopped as soon as he caught sight of the librarian. She'd just finished talking to a different officer, and in his place, another familiar face strolled over: the shopkeeper from the day before. There were a couple other women standing with them that he didn't recognize as well. The shopkeeper smiled as the librarian handed her the spell book, and as if she knew he'd be watching, she turned and met Richard's gaze.

A chill shot down his spine, and as the car started to roll away and take him down to the station, he couldn't look away from the group of women.

They were witches. Real, *evil* witches. They had the book...and there was no way to know just how big their coven was.

Made in the USA
Las Vegas, NV
13 June 2021

24701187R00031